Clever's New Trick

A social story to teach children to stop, think, and make good choices.

How to use Clever's New Trick

I began telling my little one a version of this story quite some time ago. And then I moved it into a Kindergarten classroom. And then into a different Kindergarten classroom. As it turns out, *Clever's New Trick* is a great trick for most young children to learn!

Of course there is no right or wrong way to read this story with your little one. The Teacher in me has set this book up to be rhythmic and full of rich language, so it is a great story to simply read aloud to children.

However, if you are reading this book as a social story for your little ones—a story to help support them along their journey to making friends and making good choices—then I do have some suggestions.

Talk about each step that Clever takes:

STOP—Jerome talks to Clever about the different feelings in his body he might get when he's upset: a tight feeling in his tummy, clenched hands, or a hot face. Mention to your little ones that these feelings can be thought of as 'alarm bells' or 'warning signs' that they need to stop.

THINK—throughout the book when Clever thinks, discuss with your child what choices Clever might be thinking about. Perhaps he is thinking about pushing, or getting an adult for help, or walking away. Perhaps he is going to talk to his friend, choose to play a different game, or go get a snack! There are so many choices for children to make when they are upset. This story is a great chance to chat with your little one about positive choices. It is safer for children to discuss character's choices than their own.

I hope you and your little ones enjoy Clever's New Trick!

Clever the fox walks around the edge of the forest with his shoulders slumping. He lets out a little sigh as he watches the other animals play.

How he wishes he had been invited to join in the fun!

Poor Clever. He is feeling very lonely and sad.

Just then the wise Jerome, the forest gnome, notices Clever looking a little down and decides to head over for a chat.

"What's the matter Clever? You seem a bit blue."

"None of the other animals want to play with me, Jerome. I just don't know why. Do you?"

"Hmmm ..." Jerome thought for a moment. "I just might. Clever, you are a kind Fox, but you do have trouble with your temper. When you get mad or hurt you often yell or even push. This makes the other animals feel frightened. Perhaps they are nervous to play with you."

"Oh ..." Clever said gloomily.

"But don't worry Clever. I know a trick that will help you make good choices and will let all of the animals see what a kind boy you truly are."

"A trick? That's wonderful! Please tell me."

"Do you know the feeling your body gets when you are upset? Sometimes it's a tight feeling in your tummy, or you feel your hands clench, or your face gets hot. Whenever you feel that feeling you need to STOP and count to three very slowly."

Jerome demonstrates with a great big breath and a slow count to three, 1-2-3.

"After you count to three you need to THINK. You need to think about what you can do to solve the problem that won't get anyone upset. I even have a neat craft for you to do to remember this trick."

Jerome, the forest gnome, explains the craft to Clever, but Clever decides to save the craft to do with some of the woodland animals so he doesn't feel so lonely.

Armed with his new trick, Clever bravely sets off through the woods to find some friends.

The first animal he sees is little Snowy Owl.

Snowy Owl is high in a tree when Clever calls to him inviting him down to play.

Snowy is hesitant. He knows that Clever can have a temper. But he also knows that Clever has a kind heart and some neat ideas.

He asks Clever, "What do you want to play?"

Clever looks around thoughtfully. He notices lots of loose branches on the grass that the wind has blown down.

"Why don't we build a tall tower with some of these sticks?" suggests Clever, and he begins to build.

His tower is getting taller and taller and taller!

Clever is feeling prouder and prouder and prouder!

He looks up to Snowy with a smile and once again invites her down to play.

Never one to turn down fun, Snowy decides to join in.

She swoops down to play ... but ... Oh no!

She swoops too low and knocks Clever's tower right down.

Clever gets that feeling in his tummy. He knows he is upset.

But he doesn't scream. And he doesn't push.

He STOPS and takes a very deep breath and counts to three.

Now he is calm enough to THINK.

He tells Snowy, "I know that was an accident, but I am upset. I worked hard on that tower. Would you please help me fix it?"

Snowy says, "Of course! I am sorry, I didn't mean to swoop so low. Flying is hard for me, I still have a lot to learn."

Clever thinks about that for a moment. He is surprised to hear that Snowy is still learning a skill.

Together the friends fix the tower and build it even taller than before.

Clever tells Snowy of the neat craft Jerome taught him and they decide to set off to find more friends to join them.

The next friend they meet is Pokey the Hedgehog. Pokey is busy scuffling around chasing some delicious bugs for lunch when Clever and Snowy arrive.

When Pokey sees Clever and Snowy he politely invites them to lunch.

Not being much for bugs, Clever suggests that they play tag instead.

The new friends are having lots of fun. Clever is thrilled! He is so happy to be playing with some new friends.

But then ... Oh no!

Pokey get a little too close a little too fast and pokes Clever with his quills - OUCH!

Clever feels that feeling in his tummy. This time he is hurt.

But he doesn't yell. And he doesn't hurt Pokey back.

He STOPS, takes a deep breath, and counts to three.

Then he THINKS.

He looks at Pokey, who looks very remorseful, and says, "Ouch Pokey, that hurt me! Please be more careful. Could you give me a hug to help me feel better?"

Pokey says, "Of course! I am sorry Clever, sometimes my quills get in the way of my fun. Learning to use these quills is tricky, I still have a lot to learn."

Clever liked hearing that Pokey, too, is still learning a skill.

Pokey gives Clever a careful hug and they both feel better.

Clever tells Pokey about the neat craft and the three friends decide to find one more animal to join in their craft.

The last animal they find is Flopsy Bunny. She is hopping high on a hill with her ears flip flopping all over the place!

Flopsy is a busy little bunny and always up to something fun.

In fact, just last week Flopsy and Clever had played a great game of hide the acorn. Unfortunately, Clever had lost his temper when he could not find the acorn. He yelled at Flopsy and stormed away from her and the game. But that was last week.

When Flopsy sees her woodland friends she calls to Pokey and Snowy to invite them to play.

When Clever goes along too, Flopsy says, "No! Not you Clever. You cannot play with us! Last time we played you yelled at me!"

Clever gets that feeling again. This time it feels even worse than before. He is feeling very sad and left out.

Clever almost yells at Flopsy, but he remembers his new trick.

He doesn't yell. And he doesn't scream.

Clever STOPS, takes a deep breath, and counts to three.

He THINKS really hard about what to do. He THINKS about Snowy learning to swoop and Pokey learning to be careful with his quills. He THINKS about himself learning to making good choices. Maybe Flopsy, perhaps, is a bit like him.

He calmly says to Flopsy, "Flopsy that hurts my feelings. I would really like to play too. I know sometimes I have trouble with my temper, but I have learned a neat trick and I am trying really hard to be a kind friend. I would like you to be a kind friend too and let me play."

Flopsy asks Clever about his neat trick. Clever explains how it is to help him remember to STOP and THINK.

Floppy says, "I think I need to learn that trick too Clever, I still have a lot to learn about not losing my temper and making good choices. Would you please show me the craft?"

Clever smiles. He is so happy to realize that all his new friends have things they are learning and working on, just like him.

Clever eagerly shows all of his new friends how to make the craft. This craft helps all the friends remember to STOP and THINK about choices they make.

He takes a pipe cleaner and puts on one red 'stop' bead. Next, he puts on three small, colourful 'think' beads. These bracelets will help Floppy, Clever, and all the woodland friends remember to STOP and THINK so they can make good choices.

Clever and his new friends spend the rest of the afternoon making bracelets and playing.

They all still have a lot to learn, and they will all still make mistakes, but now they know Clever's new trick to help them along their way.

Made in the USA
Middletown, DE
23 October 2018